BODY of EVIDENCE

Jeremy Brown

CRIME FILE INVESTIGATIONS

SCHOLASTIC

Scholastic Children's Books,
Euston House, 24 Eversholt Street,
London NW1 1DB, UK

A division of Scholastic Ltd
London ~ New York ~ Toronto ~ Sydney ~ Auckland
Mexico City ~ New Delhi ~ Hong Kong

First published in the US by Scholastic Inc
as the first half of *Body of Evidence*, 2005
First published in the UK by Scholastic Ltd, 2006

10 digit ISBN 0 439 95011 2
13 digit ISBN 978 0439 95011 4

10 digit ISBN 0 439 95101 1
13 digit ISBN 978 0439 95101 2

Printed and bound by Nørhaven Paperback A/S, Denmark

2 4 6 8 10 9 7 5 3 1

Papers used by Scholastic Children's Books are made from wood grown in sustainable forests.

Contents

PERSONNEL FILE

CSI Wes Burton

Burton is a witty, intelligent investigator who loves the problem-solving nature of crime scene investigation. His signature fly-fisherman's waistcoat, bristling with evidence-gathering tools, is a welcome sight at any crime scene (except those run by Detective Gibson). Not much surprises Burton, including a criminal's ability to weave a nearly perfect lie. He usually prefers evidence analysis to talking to witnesses and suspects because, unlike people, "evidence stands up; it does not lie." He appreciates Detective Radley's interviewing skills and her interest in why a crime occurred, because it allows him to focus on the how.

Detective Erin Radley

At six-foot-one, Detective Radley can be an intimidating woman. Her motto, "Convict them with kindness", seems in conflict with her physical appearance, but it is that contradiction that keeps suspects off balance and talking to her. When a woman of her stature hands you a blanket and hot chocolate, then asks why you stabbed your wife, it's hard to concentrate on your lie. Radley has a master's degree in psychology and tends to focus on the why of a case. She plans to publish a study one day on what compels criminals to commit their crimes. Working with Burton presents plenty of odd situations that will help her book stand out. She appreciates Burton's dedication to solving crimes and his ability to lighten situations that most individuals would find disturbing and depressing.

Detective Frank Gibson

Gibson is what he would call "old school", using intimidation and a loud voice to get a confession rather than patience and by-the-book techniques. In some cases his approach is required, such as when a kidnapper won't divulge the location of his latest victim, but for the most part Burton and his team do not appreciate Gibson's presence at a crime scene. Gibson and Burton constantly clash with each other, and when it comes to solving a crime, they have an unspoken competition to see who can identify the perpetrator first. The perpetrators don't stand a chance.

Mike Trellis

Trellis is Burton's CSI technician assistant. He specializes in trace analysis, arson and horrible jokes, such as commenting that a shooting victim died from "Too much lead in his diet." It doesn't help that he follows every joke with "Get it?" Burton knows that when Trellis is working on a case, he can expect close attention to detail, exhaustive analysis of evidence and dedication to finding the guilty party. Detective Gibson likes to pick on Trellis, but the young technician has a knack for frustrating the burly cop, and for that, Burton likes him even more.

Lauren Crown

Dr Crown is a shy, almost reclusive forensic pathologist. A genius in her field, she is nearly incapable of having a normal conversation. However, she is quick to recite the qualifications of a forensic pathologist should anyone refer to her as a medical examiner, or worse, a coroner. She can determine a corpse's time of death within ten minutes just by looking at it, but she has no idea who the president of the United States is – and doesn't care.

Ed

Ed, short for Exhibit D, is a search-and-rescue border collie. She was adopted and trained by Burton after being admitted as evidence in a case against her owner, a methamphetamine dealer. Her fur contained trace elements of the ingredients used to make the drug, and the dealer was convicted. She can follow ground and air scent and is in training to become a certified cadaver dog as well.

Burian U Gorlach

Burian, or Bug, as he prefers to be called, is a Russian immigrant and the owner of Sensitive

Cleaners, a company that cleans and decontaminates crime scenes when an investigation is complete. Bug is anything but sensitive, muttering in semi-English and cackling while he rips up bloodstained carpets and vacuums biohazards.

THE DEFENCE RESTS IN PEACE

CSI Wes Burton walked into the lawyer's office and immediately bristled. It wasn't seeing a corpse that disturbed him; it was the fact that he didn't see one. The dozen or so breathing people in the room were obstructing his view.

"Which one of you is dead?" he asked. A stunned silence followed as the officers, emergency medical technicians and a short, shaken woman looked at him. "If it isn't you, there's no reason for you to be at this crime scene," said Burton. Detective Erin Radley, who was used to his behaviour, tried to hide a smile.

As everyone filed out of the office, Burton took his custom-made "CRIME SCENE – DO NOT CROSS/ CRIME SEEN? STICK AROUND" yellow tape out of pocket 2 of the fly-fisherman's waistcoat he wore to every crime scene. The 30 or so other pockets on the waistcoat bulged and rattled with everything from latex gloves to a handheld ultraviolet light. He rarely came across a situation that required something that wasn't in those pockets. Radley stayed where she was, as far from the body as possible, to avoid further contaminating the scene. She had on her usual black leather jacket, and its mid-thigh length made her look even taller than usual.

One of the EMTs helped the distressed woman through the doorway. "We'll check your heart rate right away, Miss Porter. I'm sure it's nothing serious." To Burton, he said, "She has some heart-attack symptoms. If they continue, we'll have to take her to the ER."

Burton nodded. "Just keep all of her clothes, and don't let her have a shower." He stretched the yellow tape across the doorway and secured it. To him, that thin piece of plastic represented a brick wall with armed sentries on top. Maybe even a helicopter or two.

"What do we have, Detective Radley?" Burton asked as he made his way to the other side of the room, careful not to disturb anything. The two client chairs in front of the desk seemed in place, but until photographs were taken, nothing could be moved. Not moving wouldn't be a problem for Brent Cordova, former lawyer, who was face up on the floor behind his enormous desk.

"Dead lawyer," she said, opening her notepad. "Only a few million suspects."

"Shotgun to the chest?" Burton asked.

"Looks like it," Radley said. "The legal assistant, Miss Porter, says that Cordova had been planning on closing his practice and retiring next month, and he

BODY of EVIDENCE

was handing off all his defence cas
come, first-served basis. She says the
happy and have been calling with nasty m

"He didn't know making murder suspects a
can have bad side effects?" Burton asked. "Like getting murdered?"

"You'd think he would," Radley said. "Only three of his current clients are on trial for murder, and they're being tracked down right now. We'll see how their alibis look." Radley thought for a moment, then went on. "If one of them did it, I hope he'll talk to me about why."

"Are you still writing that book of yours?" Burton asked.

"Yes," she said. "I've got some fascinating stuff so far." Radley, who had a master's degree in psychology, had been compiling case studies for years that focus on why criminals commit their crimes. She planned to publish them for the law enforcement community.

"I still don't get it," Burton said. "The why doesn't prove anything. You can't convict anyone on a reason or motive; you have to know how they did it."

"True," Radley said. "But if we find out why a murder took place, maybe we can prevent the next one from happening at all."

"But people can lie about why they did something," Burton said, "and you might not be able to prove that they're lying. Evidence stands up in court. It does not lie."

"So you're always telling me," said Radley.

Burton took a closer look at the entrance wound

the body. It was on Cordova's upper left chest, ith gunshot residue and small burns on his skin and the tatters of his shirt. There was no visible exit of pellets or slugs, but from the pattern and depth of the wound, he could see that the shot had entered at a 10-degree angle from Cordova's left side, at about the height of his shoulder.

Burton also saw that Cordova's chair, a high-backed leather throne, had gunshot residue on the upper left wing. "How tall are those three murder suspects?"

Radley pulled three folders from under her arm and checked through them. "Miss Porter pulled these for me. She's pretty upset. She passed the bar exam a month ago and has helped with some of these cases. She thinks if the killer comes back, she'll be next."

"Did she witness anything?" Burton asked.

"No, she says she found him like this, called us right away. OK, here's the last one. The suspects are six-foot-three, five-foot-ten and six foot. Is that helpful?"

"Not to the shooter's case," Burton said.

The EMT stuck his head in over the crime scene tape. "Miss Porter's having some real trouble out here. Heart's racing like a jack rabbit. We're going to take her to the hospital for observation."

"That's fine," Burton said. "But let Detective Radley read her her rights first."

How did he know?

Burton's File

The entrance wound indicated that the fatal shot was close range (Gun shot residue (GSR) and burns) and came from Cordova's left. He was seated and looking straight ahead when he was shot (GSR on chair, wound on left of face rather than front), indicating that he trusted the shooter next to him. Two chairs in front of the large desk suggest all client contact is across the desk. The entrance wound angled slightly downwards, indicating that the shooter was short. A tall shooter aiming at a sitting Cordova would have produced an entrance angle nearer to 45 degrees.

Porter recently passed the bar exam, making her eligible to take over the practice, yet she was being passed over by Cordova. At the crime scene, the EMTs thought she had heart-attack symptoms: numbness or pain spreading to the shoulders, neck or arms; anxiety; nervousness; cold, sweaty skin; increased or irregular heart rate – also symptoms of recently firing a shotgun into your boss's chest.

THE BURNING QUESTION

Burton walked into the restaurant's kitchen; its stainless steel and tile surfaces were covered in soggy soot and burnt debris. The sprinklers had been shut off over an hour ago, but the overhead fixtures still dripped steadily. He brought head chef Nathan Olivo in with him, careful to keep the distraught man away from any evidence.

"I hope you like your steak well done," said Mike Trellis, Burton's CSI technician. He specialized in arson investigation and bad jokes. Burton laughed, the chef did not.

Trellis was using a fuel sniffer, which looked like a small cane attached to a lunch box, to check areas of the kitchen for traces of accelerant. Pertrol and paraffin were the most common, but he had seen arsonists use everything from Silly String to hair spray to start a fire.

"What happened here?" Burton asked.

"It was about half an hour after we closed. We were all in the bar toasting the end of the night when the kitchen just blew up. I started the toast tradition a few weeks ago when we got a mediocre review in the local restaurant guide. The toast is supposed to build morale and create team atmosphere – everyone was pretty down after that review. But the bad food wasn't our fault, it was the stove."

"The stove?" Burton said. "Was there a problem with it?"

"Problem? It was a piece of garbage," Olivo said. "Always burning entrées, scalding sauces and stinking of gas; the pilot light for one of the burners kept going out. I asked the manufacturers to replace it several times, but they refused, saying it was fine."

Trellis walked over to the blackened stove, the sniffer leading the way.

"Thank you, Mr Olivo," Burton said, leading him towards the door. "Please step outside with the other employees and we'll finish up in here."

Burton shined his flashlight around the kitchen. "The room looks like there was a sudden explosion rather than a slow burn," he said. "And soot is covering just about every surface in here – walls, counters and especially the ceiling and ceiling fans – so whatever happened, it sent residue everywhere. But what burned in order to make the soot? Soot results from imperfect burning, and gas burns cleanly, with no residue. I can't believe the kitchen had enough dust to cause this mess." Burton looked again at the ceiling and the black film covering it.

"Wait a minute. Were the ceiling fans on when the kitchen blew?"

Trellis checked his notes. "The fan switch was in the on position, but the explosion knocked out the electricity, so they weren't spinning for long. The big exhaust ducts up there were off for the night."

"Let's try to get a fingerprint off of that fan switch," Burton said. He climbed onto the stainless steel island in the middle of the kitchen and took a closer look at one of the ceiling fans. It was caked with black soot, as was the ceiling above it. He reached above the fan and ran his finger along the top side of one of the blades. It came back with a white substance on it. Burton smelled it once, then touched it to his tongue.

"Mmm. Tastes like arson," he said.

How did he know?

Burton's File

Olivo's claim that the faulty stove caused the explosion could not have been true. The amount of soot in the room indicated an accelerant other than the gas from the stove, and the amount of residue on the ceiling and ceiling fans showed that a large amount of the accelerant was near the top of the room; the fans would have blown gas away from the ceiling.

The staff was out of the kitchen for 30 minutes when the explosion occurred; a leaking pilot light would require much more time to fill the kitchen with enough gas to cause the explosion.

Olivo wanted to blame his restaurant's poor review on the defective stove; instead he proved how good he was at burning things. He waited until his staff was safe in the bar, then turned on the ceiling fans, on which he had piled an accelerant that can easily be found in any kitchen: flour. In dust form, flour and other grains are explosive, something a chef would have known. Once the dust drifted down to the pilot lights, it was kitchen flambé.

CRIME FILE INVESTIGATIONS

NO DAY AT THE BEACH

Burton read the print-out from the gas chromatograph/mass spectrometer and nodded. The two samples he had submitted to the machine for analysis were from the steering wheel and driver's seat of Charlotte Haney's car. What was left of it, anyway. A 250-foot fall into a ravine full of boulders tends to do more than scuff the bumper.

As he expected, the samples were identical, with high amounts of zinc oxide and titanium dioxide. Burton made his way back to the interview room and entered to find Detective Frank Gibson questioning Ted Haney, Charlotte's husband and the only witness to the accident. Gibson was a bully and had a reputation for getting confessions before the crime lab could even sweep the scene. He claimed it saved him paperwork. Burton didn't particularly like his methods, but he saw their usefulness in some situations. Burton had a bit of a reputation himself; something to do with not liking bullies and lazy detectives.

"I already told you," Ted sputtered. "She got into the car to get the camera, and it started rolling. She was leaning in through the door of the backseat, so she couldn't tell the car was moving, and—"

"At what point did you start to push the car?" Detective Gibson interrupted. "Or did you just knock her unconscious and take your time rolling it over the cliff?"

"Hold on there, Detective," Burton said. "Mr Haney is a witness, not a suspect. If he becomes a suspect, we have to bring in the really bright light and crank the thermostat up to 110 degrees. You know that. Look at him, he's already sweating."

"What's your problem, Burton? Did you run out of pink outline chalk or something?" Gibson said with a sneer.

"Don't worry," Burton said as he sat down. "I finished your hopscotch squares first."

Before Gibson could think of a retort, Burton handed Haney a paper towel, then took it back when the man had finished wiping his face and hands. He leaned back and put it in the rubbish bin, but not in the rubbish bag. Instead, he placed it in an evidence bag he had taped to the inside of the rim before Haney had entered the room. He closed the evidence bag, then the rubbish bag, and handed them to Gibson.

"Here, Frank. You always talk about how you want to clean up this town. Start with this room." Gibson looked as though he'd rather put the bag over

Burton's head, but he snatched it away and slammed the door.

"Mr Haney, you said that you and your wife spent the morning and early afternoon at the beach, then stopped on the way home to take some pictures from the lookout. Charlotte drove the entire time?"

"That's right," Haney said. His reddish face indicated to Burton that Haney wasn't too concerned about getting sunburned. He recounted the entire story, obviously shaken by the event and needing to talk it through.

As he listened, Burton peered into his file at the accident photographs, careful to keep them out of Haney's view. Charlotte's body, also tanned and sunburned, was damaged beyond recognition. However, with Ted at the scene as the accident occurred, no body identification was necessary. After 15 minutes, Gibson returned and stood behind Haney. He had a print-out in his hand, the results of the crime lab analysis of the paper towels. Gibson gave Burton a slight shake of his head. There was no zinc oxide or titanium dioxide on the paper towel Haney used.

Burton closed the file folder. "OK, Mr Haney, I just have one more question. Where is Charlotte now, and why does she want us to think she's dead?"

How did Burton know?

Burton's File

The chemicals found on the steering wheel and driver's seat of Charlotte Haney's car, zinc oxide and titanium dioxide, are found in sunscreen. Whoever had been driving the car wore sunscreen. The paper towel Ted Haney used did not have any traces of those chemicals, which means that he did not apply the sunscreen to himself or another person. The body in the car was tanned and sunburned, too, signifying that no sunscreen had been applied recently enough to transfer onto the steering wheel and car seat. Charlotte Haney is alive and well somewhere, and she is wearing sunscreen.

CRIME FILE INVESTIGATIONS

WITH DEADLIEST REGARDS

"Well, this all looks very fancy and fun," Detective Gibson said as he entered the interview room. Burton was sitting across the table from Lionel Walker, an antiques dealer who happened to be wearing a nineteenth-century tuxedo and top hat.

"Yes," Burton said. "Mr Walker is fancy, and I'm having fun, and now that you're here, we can add 'foolish' to the mix. Now I'm having even more fun. Are you having fun, Mr Walker?"

"Most certainly not!" Walker sputtered. His white moustache bristled when he spoke, and Burton half expected an antique eyeglass to drop from his incredulous eye.

"You're not here to have fun," Gibson said, leaning onto the table. "You're here to confess to the murder of your sweetheart, Rebecca Shuman. So let's get it over with."

Walker refused to look at Gibson, and he spoke deliberately to Burton. "Good sir, would you be so kind as to remove this Neanderthal from my presence? He's making the very air unbreathable."

"Neanderthal?" Gibson said. "What's that, like a caveman? Listen here, frills, I wish we were in caveman times, because instead of a trial, you'd just get pushed off a cliff and forgotten. In fact, I think there's a cliff just down the road." Gibson took a step closer to Walker, who pulled his top hat off and held it in front of himself like a shield.

"Back, you idiot!" Walker shouted.

"All right, calm down," Burton said. "Mr Walker, our forensic pathologist is examining the deceased Ms Shuman right now. If there's anything you'd like to tell us before we find out for ourselves, it could help you out in court."

"The Lady Shuman and I do have a past," Walker said, keeping a wary eye on Gibson. "But we parted ways months ago and haven't spoken since then. I do pine for her, though, and send her antique artificial flowers now and again. They were her favourite. I regret her passing as if it were my own."

Gibson rolled his eyes. "Where did you find this guy, Burton? The Melodrama Store?"

"Good one, Frank," Burton said. "You should write it down and use it again. You two play nicely, I'm going to see how Dr Crown is doing." As Burton left, he saw Gibson smile at Walker and thought he saw Walker begin to sweat.

Dr Lauren Crown was the county's forensic pathologist, and that was just about all Burton knew about her. He had the feeling that if she could examine the bodies without leaving her garage, which she had converted into a home lab and library, she would. He entered the crime lab and found Mike Trellis assisting Dr Crown in the examination of Rebecca Shuman.

"Hey, boss," Trellis said. "Check out her fingernails. Dr Crown spotted it straight away when she heard that Shuman had vomited several times before she died."

Burton looked at the corpse's fingernails and saw the white lines and horizontal ridges. "Arsenic poisoning?" he asked.

"Correct," Dr Crown said without looking away from her microscope.

"Did hair analysis have traces of arsenic, too?"

"Yes," Crown said, and pointed to a print-out on the table. Burton looked at the print-out.

"Looks like she's been in contact with the poison for at least a few months, maybe longer," he said.

"Yes," Crown said, and picked up a bone saw.

Burton and Trellis waited for more comments from her, but she continued what she was doing without giving them a glance.

"Should we make small talk with her or just leave?" Trellis asked Burton quietly.

"I don't know," Burton answered. "Do you want to talk about advanced states of decomposition and what various forms of trauma can do to an eyeball?"

"No," Trellis said. "No, I don't. What about football?" Burton considered it, then made a face.

"Not likely," he said. "We'll probably have more luck talking to Gibson."

Burton and Trellis went back to the interview room, where Gibson was sitting on the table and Walker was sitting in the corner.

"Bad news, Mr Walker," Trellis said. "You've been nailed."

What gave Walker away?

Burton's File

Walker mentioned that he had been sending artificial antique flowers to Rebecca Shuman since they broke up. As an antiques dealer, Walker would have known that many nineteenth-century items, including artificial flowers, playing cards and hat liners, contained lethal amounts of arsenic. He sent the flowers to her knowing she would spread them around her home, surrounding herself with poison.

CRIME FILE INVESTIGATIONS

THE NOSE KNOWS

It was a chilly day, and Burton pulled his knitted cap down over his ears as he approached the group of reporters. They were crowded around Carol Morrell, who was on the verge of tears. Her son, Brandon, stood next to her, trying to console his mother. Burton guessed his age to be 13.

"Please, if you know where my daughter is, call me, or the police, or anyone! She's only four years old! She—" Mrs Morrell broke down then, the news cameras catching every second of her despair.

"All right, everyone," Burton said, "we're about to begin searching for Janie Morrell, so we need you to clear the area. Back to your vans, please."

Carol and Brandon stayed put, Carol wiping her eyes. "Please," she said. "Janie couldn't have gone too far, but Brandon and I can't find her. We stopped to pick up some autumn leaves, and I took my eyes off her for a second, just a second. You don't think someone ... took her, do you?" The tears welled back up, and she hid her face in her hands.

"We'll find her, Mrs Morrell, don't worry," Burton said. "I'm Wes Burton, from the scene investigation department." He left out the word "crime," as he wasn't sure there was a crime yet, and the word sometimes upset people. "I'd like to establish a timeline before we get started. You left your home at 7.00 am and stopped at this field to collect leaves around 8.00 am; you noticed Janie was missing approximately ten minutes after that and called the police. Then at 8.23, the first officer arrived on scene. He asked you to stop talking to the reporters and make a statement, in case there was information that we could use to find Janie. It is now 8.37, so she's been missing for almost 30 minutes. Is that all correct?"

"I guess," Carol said. "I'm not sure about the times, things were crazy. I thought talking to the reporters would help, since more people would know she's missing and could look for her."

"Thank you, Mrs Morrell," Burton said. "I'll go and get my partner, Ed, and we'll get to work finding your daughter." Burton made his way back to his truck, stopping on the way to check the Morrell minivan. The bonnet was cool to the touch, the driver's door open from when Carol made her emergency call. Burton found what he was looking for and headed for his partner.

"I checked your minivan and found a good scent article that will help us track Janie," Burton said when he returned.

"Your partner uses his nose to find people?" Brandon asked, temporarily distracted from his worry.

"Ed is a she, and she's a border collie," Burton explained. "Her name's short for Exhibit D. I adopted her after a trial a few years ago, and she does search-and-rescue with me. Here she comes. Would you like to meet her?"

Brandon nodded as Ed burst from the bushes, her coat tangled with burrs and her tongue flopping happily. Her orange search-and-rescue vest had bells sewn onto the back to help Burton follow her in the woods, and the chimes sang as she bounded towards the group.

"Come on, Ed!" Burton called. "Let's meet Brandon. We're going to find his sister Janie this morning!" Ed thought that was a great idea and let Brandon know by giving him a quick lick on the hand as he scratched her ears.

"OK, Mrs Morrell," Burton said. "You and Brandon can follow, but stay at least 50 yards behind me to keep the scent clean." With that, Burton turned his back and knelt next to Ed. He pulled a sealed plastic bag with something in it out of waistcoat pocket 4, let Ed get a whiff, and off she went. Her nose worked furiously as she followed the scent that matched the item in the bag.

"Here we go," Burton said. "Remember, stay behind me; I'll shout when Ed finds her."

Carol nodded, clearly anxious to see her daughter again. "Brandon, let's go and get my mittens and your gloves. Mr Burton should be far enough ahead by then." Her tone suggested that she resented being left out of the front lines, but Burton wasn't about to budge. He followed Ed, who was tracking the ground scent into the trees.

It only took 12 minutes for Ed to find Janie, who was sitting by the trunk of a tree waving a stick around. Burton arrived soon after and made sure the little girl was safe and warm. He radioed to the officers escorting the Morrells that Janie was safe and told them it was OK to come and get her.

"Oh, thank goodness!" Carol gasped as she lifted Janie off the ground and into a hug. The mother wore one red mitten on her right hand, which she took off to touch her daughter's face. "Thank you, Mr Burton, and thank you, Ed. I don't know how long she would have been out here if you hadn't followed her scent!"

"You're welcome, Mrs Morrell. But when your kids are safe, you'll have to come with us," Burton said as he pulled the bag out of his pocket. In it was the other red mitten. "Ed didn't follow Janie's scent out here. She followed yours."

How did he know?

Burton's File

When the first officer arrived on scene, the reporters were already there, indicating that Carol Morrell had called them first, something a terrified mother would not do. If the van had been off for 40 minutes, as Carol claimed, the bonnet would still be warm to the touch after driving for a full hour. That meant she had been stopped for a longer period of time. Long enough, in fact, for her to take Janie into the woods, tell her to stay there, and run back to her van and call the news channels and the police. Carol just wanted some attention – the judge will give her plenty.

CRIME FILE INVESTIGATIONS

THE SCENE'S ABUZZ

"Bug wants to talk to you," Detective Radley said to Burton.

"Do you have any idea why?" Burton responded as he packed away the last of his equipment. They had just finished processing a murder scene at the Rider's Lodge Motel, and Burton was hot and upset. The victim was unidentified, the room hadn't been let to anyone during the time of the murder, and they hadn't been able to find much of anything in the way of evidence.

"Because you're the only one who can understand what he's talking about," she offered. Bug, or Burian U Gorlach, was a recent immigrant from Russia. He owns Sensitive Cleaners, a company that specializes in the cleaning and decontamination of crime scenes when an investigation is complete. He was currently in room 41, where the murder took place.

"Good point," Burton said, and made his way to room 41.

"Ah, Wes Burtons, goods to see you!" Bug said, when Burton appeared in the doorway. He was standing near the middle of the room in a Tyvek suit, next to a large bloodstain in the carpet.

"Hello, Bug, good to see you, too. You must be hot in that suit. It's close to 35 degrees outside," Burton said.

"Yes, I am in fire," Bug said.

"What can I do for you?" Burton asked.

"I am thinking, I am good at cleaner of the stains of blood and filth, yes?" Bug said.

"One of the best I've ever seen," Burton said. And it was true; Bug was exceptionally thorough when it came to cleaning a messy crime scene.

"Da, da, but even I am not this good," Bug said, and pulled back the carpet. The underside of the carpet showed the back side of the bloodstain, indicating that the fluid had soaked through, but the concrete floor underneath was spotless.

"You didn't touch the concrete at all?" Burton asked, his interest immediately spiking.

"No, I just look at it, and it is already clean," Bug said. "I'm wishing my job is always this easy!"

Burton radioed to Detective Radley, and she arrived a few minutes later, along with the motel manager. "There's no blood on the concrete below the carpet stain," Burton explained. "I think the murder took place in another motel room, and the killer swapped the carpet pieces. That's why there wasn't any evidence in this room. The way this place is laid out, every second room is identical." He stopped suddenly and looked at the manager. "How many rooms do you have?" he asked.

"Two hundred," the manager replied, wary of where the conversation was leading.

"So there are 100 rooms with the same floor plan as this one, leaving 99 other possible murder scenes here," Burton said to Radley.

"Whoa, whoa, hold on there," the manager said. "I can't have you shutting me down while you peel up half of my carpets! Just removing the furniture will take all day!"

"That won't be necessary," Burton said. "Just open the other 99 doors and wait about one hour."

Why didn't Burton need to pull up every carpet?

Burton's File

In the near 35-degree heat, the bloodstain on the concrete quickly attracted houseflies and blowflies. They are the first insects to arrive when a body starts to decay. Bug discovered the concrete was missing a bloodstain in room 41. Real bugs found the bloodstain for us in another room.

CRIME FILE INVESTIGATIONS

THE SWIRLY GIG

"Sit down," Burton said for the second time. Across the interview table from him, 21-year-old Ronnie Warren smirked and remained standing.

"You sit down," Ronnie said.

Burton frowned. "I am sitting down."

"Good for you."

"Do you consider this to be an actual conversation?" Burton asked.

"No, but you do."

"Sit down," said Burton.

"I don't have to sit down," Ronnie said. "I know my rights, and when my lawyer gets here, you'll be the one taking orders."

Detective Erin Radley moved around the table and stood next to Ronnie. She wore her favourite leather jacket, the dark, smooth leather a close match to her skin. Ronnie shifted slightly, apparently not very comfortable with a six-foot-one-inch woman looking down at him. She smiled, which made him more uncomfortable.

"Sit down, hon," she said. And he sat down.

"Wow," Burton said. "Are you going to put that in your book?"

Radley gave a modest shrug. "Why give away all my secrets?"

"What book?" Ronnie asked suspiciously.

"I'm compiling case studies on why criminals commit their crimes," Radley explained. "Perhaps you'd like to speculate on why you killed Tim Keenan?"

Ronnie paused, then a sly grin appeared. "Oh no, you're not going to trick me that easily!"

"Is that what you think we're trying to do?" Radley asked. "Trick you? Believe me, we don't want you to confess. We would rather see the long-drawn-out process of an indictment, a trial, appeals..."

"Don't forget the interrogations," Burton chimed in.

"Oh, yes, the interrogations," Radley said, and smiled at Ronnie again. The young man looked uncertain about the whole situation.

Before Radley and Burton could continue their conversation, Mike Trellis opened the door, followed by another man.

"This is Travis Beckman, the lawyer," Trellis said.

"That's how I'm introduced?" Beckman spat. "'The lawyer'? Like I'm some kind of professional wrestler?"

Trellis seemed to be distracted by this image, so Beckman turned his attention to Burton and Radley. "Whatever my client has said so far is inadmissible in court. He did not have proper representation at the time. And why is he wearing a jumpsuit? Has he been convicted already?"

"We confiscated everyone's clothes for examination," Burton said. "Mr Warren is here regarding the death of Tim Keenan. They were team-mates on a football team. They were playing a game at the park, when Ronnie and a few other players took a time-out to give Tim a swirly – that's push his head down the toilet and flush it. He died."

"That's not true!" said Ronnie. "We were going to dunk him, and he just passed out—"

"Ronnie, hush," Beckman said, laying a hand on his client's arm.

Trellis held a folder in his hand and motioned for Burton to join him in the hall. Radley stayed in the room with the three men, still smiling, with her arms crossed.

"Crown just finished her examination," Trellis said. "Tim Keenan didn't drown; there was no water in his lungs. He died from postural asphyxia."

"His chest was compressed, making him unable to breathe?" Burton asked, scanning the notes in the folder.

"Righto," said Trellis. "She also found traces of a substance containing menthol. She took some photos, yeah, right there."

Burton pulled the images out of the folder. One showed Tim Keenan's back, with close-ups indicating the menthol substance around his kidneys. Another showed a pair of tracksuit bottoms, with the same substance on the back of the thighs.

"Are these Ronnie's?" Burton asked.

"Yessir," Trellis said.

"Well," said Burton. "We won't need a chair for this evidence; it'll stand up in court."

"Good deal," said Trellis. "So, did Ronnie flush his life down the toilet? Get it?

"Yeah, I get it, Mike," Burton said and left him in the hall.

"Am I going to miss the game this Friday? It's the league championship," Ronnie said to his lawyer.

"No, we'll be leaving right now, so this farce won't affect your playing time. Right?" Beckman directed this question at Burton, who shrugged.

"It shouldn't, as long as he can throw a football with handcuffs on."

How did Burton know?

Burton's File

Tim Keenan died from postural asphyxia, death by suffocation due to the position of the body or compression of the chest. Keenan also had menthol smeared on his lower back, a common ingredient in ointments for soothing muscle and joint pain, something a football player would have. The same substance was found on the back of Ronnie Warren's trousers, indicating that he was sitting on Keenan's back while attempting to dunk his head in the toilet bowl. Keenan suffocated because his chest was pinned between Warren and the rim of the bowl.

CRIME FILE INVESTIGATIONS

DIRTY LAUNDRY

CSI technician Mike Trellis entered the interview room with a basket of clothes. His wire-framed glasses were crooked, and he set the basket down as soon as he could in order to straighten them. Trellis believed everything should be in its place all of the time. It was a philosophy that kept his laboratory neat, but it also made it easy for his peers to drive him crazy. Peers like Wes Burton.

Burton dumped the clothes basket onto the interview table and scattered the laundry across the surface. Trellis clenched his jaw, his hand involuntarily twitching towards the clothes to put them back in the basket.

"Help me sort these, will you, Mike?" Burton asked, shoving the darks into one pile and the whites into another. Trellis began to fold one of the white T-shirts, and Burton snatched it from his hands and held it in front of Ben Reeves, the suspect in the interview chair.

"You say you were doing laundry when the robbery occurred," Burton said. "Did this shirt make it into the clean pile?"

"I already told you," Reeves sighed. "I washed everything. It's all clean. You took that shirt out of the dryer yourself, I saw you. Go ahead, smell it."

Burton put the shirt near his nose and sniffed. "Hmm. It is fresh like morning dew. What do you think, Mike?" Burton held the shirt for Trellis while the technician leaned closer.

"Smells like a meadow at dawn," Trellis said, his face unchanged.

"See?" Reeves exclaimed. "There's no way I could have robbed that greeting-card shop next door. I was too busy washing all my clothes."

"You could have left while they were in the dryer," Burton said. "Robbed the card shop, then returned to your laundry before we arrived."

"Yeah, you could have really taken that card shop to the cleaners," Trellis added. "Get it?"

"No, I don't get it," Reeves said. "I wouldn't have left my stuff there. Especially my soap; that stuff's expensive. People have taken it before, and as you can see, that's not exactly a crime-free neighbourhood."

Burton pulled a large orange container from the basket and set it in front of Reeves. The bottle read "Flow-Plus — Now with bleach alternative!"

"Is this your detergent? The detergent you used today?" Burton asked.

"Yeah, it's good stuff. You smelled it. It's good, right?" Reeves said.

"I'd use it," Trellis said as he turned off the overhead lights, leaving the room in darkness.

"That's a big compliment," Burton said in the blackness. "Mike is very picky about his soaps."

Reeves flinched as Trellis turned on his handheld UV light, casting a hazy purple glow throughout the room.

"This is ultraviolet light," Trellis said. "Sometimes called UV for short, or black light. We use it to find traces of substances on fabrics and other surfaces. I'm just going to quickly check your laundry and your hands."

Trellis swept the light over the piles of laundry. The darks had a few pieces of fluff that glowed dully, while the whites offered a flat greyish-white colour.

"Nothing," the technician said, snapping the UV light off and the overheads back on.

"See?" Reeves said. "There's nothing. Can I go now?"

"Sure," Burton said. "You can go and make your one phone call."

How did they know?

Burton's File

The detergent Reeves claimed to have used that day contained a "bleach alternative." When exposed to ultraviolet light, bleach, bleach alternatives and white fabrics that have been washed in them, glow brightly. Reeves's whites were a dull grey, indicating that they had not been washed with that detergent in the recent past.

Reeves put his clothes in the dryer, went next door and robbed the greeting-card shop. He was back with his laundry before the police arrived.

CRIME FILE INVESTIGATIONS

BADD: BURTON AGAINST DEAD DRIVERS

"This is a tough tree," Trellis said, gazing up the four-foot-wide trunk to the top of the oak. It was at least 50 feet tall. The trunk was also stuck in the bonnet of a four-door sedan, the silver bumper bent around the tree like a piece of macaroni.

"It's probably seen worse than this during a windstorm," Burton said as he finished taking photos. "The driver, however, would disagree." The man slumped behind the steering wheel had been pronounced dead by the first emergency medical technicians on scene. Burton leaned into the front seat for a closer look.

"Broken nose, lacerations on the forehead, most likely from the impact with the windscreen," he said. "No seat belt."

Trellis made a tsking sound, reprimanding the corpse for ignoring simple safety precautions. Burton panned his torch over the windscreen. It was cracked in a spider-web pattern, shatter lines spreading out from the centre.

"Where's the blood?" he asked.

Trellis checked the same areas, then placed his beam on the driver's face. "A broken nose typically bleeds quite a bit," he said. "Could he have died instantly, stopping the heart and blood flow?"

"There would still be blood in the capillaries and tissues," Burton said. "And if the impact with the windscreen killed him, there would be blood on the glass for sure." He swept his torch down the body, stopping at the feet and the accelerator pedal.

"I've got some dust on and around the accelerator pedal," said Burton. He took some adhesive lifting tape out of waistcoat pocket 7. He smoothed the lifting tape over the carpet below the pedal and sealed it away, then did the same on the pedal with another tape and sealed up that one. He held the two transparent sheets up for examination.

"Looks like bits of concrete," Trellis said.

"I agree, but we'll test it to make sure," said Burton. "Check the bottoms of his shoes for more." He handed Trellis two footprint-lifting tapes from pocket 21.

Trellis extended both of the driver's legs towards the pedals and shone his light onto the soles of his shoes. "I don't see any concrete, but it's hard to tell from this angle."

"Wait a minute," Burton said. "His feet don't reach the pedals."

Trellis looked at the man's feet, then the accelerator and brake pedals. "Huh," he said.

"When it comes to driving this car, he comes up a little short. Get it?"

"Yeah, good one," Burton said. "Take some photos and a video of his feet and their distance from the pedals, then you can take the shoes off."

Trellis worked both cameras, then pulled the shoes off without untying them. He carefully pressed them onto the large lifting tapes. "I see some hair, what looks like possible dog poop, and bits of grit, but no concrete," he said.

"Call dispatch," Burton said. "Tell them this car accident just became the dump site of a murder victim."

"Are you sure?" Trellis said.

"Do you remember what I said about building a case with evidence?" Burton asked Trellis.

"Sure," Trellis answered. "It's like building a house, one piece of evidence at a time, using them like bricks until you have a solid foundation to base the case upon."

"Exactly," Burton said. "And right now, we need to find that first brick. And I mean an actual brick."

How did Burton know?

Burton's File

When a body dies, the blood begins to clot almost immediately. The lack of blood spatter on the windscreen and the driver's body indicated that the wounds he suffered in the car accident were postmortem; he was already dead. When Trellis pulled the driver's feet towards the pedals to check for concrete bits, it was apparent that the driver could not have reached the pedals. That fact, combined with the traces of concrete found on the floor and the accelerator pedal, suggests that a brick was used to press the pedal while the dead driver went along for the ride.

CRIME FILE INVESTIGATIONS

THE HALLOWEEN EGG SCENE

Burton sat on his front steps. Blood oozed from multiple gashes on his face and one eye dangled from its socket. A ninja, a tramp and a princess walked up his path, got one look at him and stopped. For a moment, anyway – then the huge bowl of sweets in his lap convinced them to approach.

"Trick or treat!" the tramp said, his worldly belongings stuffed into a handkerchief tied to a stick. The other two echoed him, as their waiting father watched and smiled.

"I think I might have a treat or three for you," Burton said in a scratchy, sinister voice. "Chocolate or fruity?"

"Chocolate!" they all shouted. He gave them each a handful of assorted mini chocolate bars, then leaned in. They leaned back.

"Say, you kids haven't seen my pet alien around here, have you?" he asked.

"No," said the princess.

"Geez, I just saw him a minute ago," Burton said. "If he gets lost, I think my heart might break." Suddenly, a small, snarling creature burst out of Burton's chest, and he bellowed in agony. The three trick-or-treaters screamed and ran off into their father's arms, laughing hysterically. The father gave Burton a thumbs-up, which he returned as he reset the spring-loaded latex alien strapped to his chest. He helped himself to another chocolate bar, careful not to mess up his bloody face.

As soon as he heard Mrs Wendell shouting four houses down the street, he was off the steps and on his way over to her house, with Ed right next to him on a lead. When he got to Mrs Wendell's garden, he was careful to avoid the waist-high shrubs that ran along the street; her cats liked to use them as a toilet. Ed hung back for a few sniffs but moved on after a light tug from Burton. Mrs Wendell was standing in her front garden.

"What's wrong, Mrs Wendell?" Burton said. "We heard you all the way from our place."

"Punks!" Mrs Wendell said through gritted teeth. "They asked for candy, and when I gave them a piece each, they asked for more! I told them there were more kiddies on the way, so I had to make sure I had enough candy for them. And what do these kids do? They egg my house!" Burton could see the shattered shells and running yolks on her door.

"Then they ran through my good bushes," Mrs Wendell cried. She pointed to the shrubs along the road. "What I wouldn't give to have them come back for more candy! I'd give them garlic and liver wrapped in wax paper!"

"How about if I just get them to come back and clean up the mess they made?" Burton said.

"Oh, I'd make them do that, too," Mrs Wendell said. "One of them left this plastic machete behind. Guess he couldn't hold it and pelt my house at the same time. Will it help you catch them?"

"What do you think, Ed?" Burton asked the perk-eared Border collie. "Do you want to do some work?" Ed responded with furious tail wagging. Burton led her to the street side of the bushes. Burton held the plastic machete by the blade and offered her the handle, which she sniffed once. Then she was off.

Burton let her take her lead to its full length and trotted behind her. After a few lefts and rights, Burton spotted a group of teenagers at the end of the street. Ed led him right to them, then sat down and looked at Burton, which was her signal that she had found the source of the scent. He gave her a biscuit and scratched her ears.

"Excuse me," Burton said to the group and showed his badge. "I'm CSI Wes Burton. Can I ask you a few questions?"

"Um, I guess," said a werewolf.

"My neighbour's house just got vandalized by a group about your size," Burton said. "If it was you, and you come back and clean it up right now, we won't have to call the police."

"We didn't egg that lady's house!" protested a girl wearing a headset microphone and loads of make-up.

“What are you supposed to be?” Burton asked. “The person at the fast-food drive-through?”

“I’m a pop star!” she yelled.

“Oh, right,” Burton said, and looked at Ed. She looked back at him and panted; she didn’t see the resemblance either.

Burton pulled out a handheld black light, snapped it on and stepped closer to the group. They stepped back in unison. “I’m just going to check for something,” Burton said. “Hold still for three seconds.” He swept the UV light across the group at their shins and saw greenish yellow streaks glowing on their trouser legs.

“Cool! I’m radioactive!” said a zombie.

“Well, zombie,” Burton said. “Call your undead, radioactive parents and get them to pick you up at Mrs Wendell’s house in about an hour. It should take that long to clean up the mess you made.”

How did Burton know it was them?

Burton's File

Ed tracking the scent to them was enough evidence to contact the police. However, it wouldn't convince the parents or get the kids to confess, so the situation required the use of an old detective's trick. At the mention that someone had vandalized a neighbour's house, one of the suspects responded with information she could only know if she had been there: eggs were used and it was a woman's house.

When the group fled the scene, they ran through Mrs Wendell's "good" bushes, which contain a large amount of cat urine. Cat urine glows under black light, and the streaks on their trousers showed they had run through the shrubbery. Case closed.

CRIME FILE INVESTIGATIONS

GAMER OVER

Burton and Detective Gibson stepped into The Gamer's Dungeon and both immediately took off their sunglasses. "Won't be needing these in here," Burton said.

"Nah," said Tom "Nebular" Evans, the owner of the Internet café and multiplayer gaming centre. "I keep it midnight dark in here around the clock. It cuts down on eye fatigue from monitor glare." He took a large gulp of some sort of coffee drink.

"What happens when people leave here after a few hours and hit the bright sunshine?" Detective Gibson asked.

"Oh, man, it's great," Evans said as he took them deeper into the Dungeon. "It's like watching vampires burn up from the sun. Except for the burning part. There's a lot of cringing and shouting. And you said 'a few hours.' Make it more like ten."

“Kids are in here for ten or more hours playing video games?” Burton asked, wishing he still had his sunglasses on so they could hide his surprise.

“Oh, yeah, and not just kids,” Evans said with pride. “We have an over-thirty league that plays every Thursday, but they don’t stay as late. Jobs.” He said the word like it was his number-one competitor and gulped more coffee.

“Are these kids drinking caffeine the whole time they’re here?” Burton asked.

“Some do, some don’t,” Evans said. “Some of them prefer energy drinks, which I also sell. I drink the hard stuff, double espressos. Make ’em myself.” He tipped the mug to his mouth, emptying it.

“Let me guess,” Gibson said, pointing into the far corner of the gaming room. “That’s our dead guy.” The people in the room had moved away from the figure slumped over his keyboard, but they hadn’t stopped playing.

“Yeah, that’s Trogdor139,” Evans said. “No one knows for sure, but we think he’s been like that for about an hour.”

“Has anyone left this room since you discovered the body?” Burton asked.

“No,” Evans said. “In fact, I think three more players have joined up since then.” Gibson turned on his huge Maglite torch and lit up the immediate area while Burton took photos.

“Hey!” a voice shouted from close by.

“Shaddup!” Gibson offered as an apology.

Burton saw a black jacket hanging on the back of Trogdor139’s chair and gently reached into the pockets, looking for identification. In the second pocket he found a prescription bottle.

"Lortox," Burton read. "This is medication for high blood pressure, or hypertension. The EMTs said they thought he died of a stroke, which would make sense if he had high blood pressure."

"So our guy had some stress from playing video games all day," Gibson said. "Rough life. Looks like he wasn't too careful about it, though." Gibson indicated the six empty and one half-full espresso mugs next to Trogdor139.

"Yeah, he wasn't too careful of his health," Evans said.

"Who was sitting closest to, uh, Trogdor?" Burton asked. "Before they found out he was dead."

"I think it was PixieDust56," Evans said. "She's over there. I'll go and get her."

"Of course, PixieDustBall999 or whatever her name is," Gibson said to Burton. "Sounds like a robot. Can't wait to meet her."

Evans returned with a short, thin girl in a black T-shirt and maroon knitted cap pulled down almost to her eyes. She wore headphones around her neck, and Burton could hear something loud and clanging coming from them.

"Hello, I'm Wes Burton, from the crime lab. Can I call you something besides PixieDust?"

"Laura," she said.

"OK, Laura, can you tell us anything about what Trogdor here was doing before he died?"

"Well," she said. "He's always, like, pounding the mouse and keyboard, swearing and stuff.

The newbies don't like to play when he's in the game. He's a camper and a TK'er."

"A what and a what now?" Gibson said.

Evans answered. "A camper is a player who finds a good hiding spot and sits there, not moving, killing players as they pass by. TK stands for Team Killer, someone who kills team-mates on purpose. Trogdor139 was notorious for both, and I've had plenty of players leave because of him. He always taunted them because they couldn't kill him."

"Was he doing these things today?" Burton asked Laura.

"Oh, yeah, like big-time," she said. "And he was like, shaking and acting all dizzy, like he kept wanting to tip over?"

"Is that a question or a statement?" Gibson asked.

"Um, a statement?" Laura said.

"Please continue, Laura," Burton said.

"Anyway," she said. "He was messing with his headphones for, like, a half hour. He said he couldn't understand what they were saying. Then he really started freaking out, like half of his body wouldn't work. Then he fell on his keyboard and, like, died, I guess."

"Did you notice him getting worse as he drank these espressos?" Burton asked, pointing to the cups on the table.

"I guess, but he only drank decaf," Laura said. "He said caffeine was a crutch."

"Thank you for your time, Laura," Burton said. "You can go back to playing, but please don't leave just yet." When she left, Burton turned to Gibson.

“I need to bag those coffee cups and the Lortox for testing.”

To Evans, he said, “I think congratulations are in order. You finally killed Trogdor139.”

How did Burton know?

Burton's File

Evans said that he made all of the coffee drinks himself, but when Gibson noticed the empty cups near Trogdor139, Evans did not mention that they were decaf, because they weren't. Trogdor139's behaviour cost Evans customers and money. He switched the player to regular espresso in an attempt to disrupt his game. When the surge of caffeine increased Trogdor139's dangerously high blood pressure, he had a stroke and died.

CRIME FILE INVESTIGATIONS

WATER YOU TRYING TO PROVE

"Are you sure that's a person?" Trellis asked Dr Crown.

"Female for certain, age is undetermined at this point," Crown answered. The body recovered from Two Mile Lake had been underwater for at least a few days and the decomposition was advanced.

"I checked recent reports," Burton said. "There was a missing-person report filed two days ago for Alyssa Taylor, who lives about half a mile from the lake."

"Do you have any DNA samples for comparison?" Crown asked.

"Her husband's on the way here with a hairbrush and her razor," Burton said. "It sounded like he'd rather keep hoping she's alive than get this kind of closure."

"Man, she's like a big sponge," Trellis said to no one in particular.

"Some people call it superhydration," Crown said. "Think about when you have your hands in water for an extended period of time. The thick skin on your palms and fingers swells up, but it's connected to a layer of skin beneath that doesn't swell, so the skin buckles, or prunes. Now imagine your whole body being submerged for days and the different ways your tissues would react."

"Thanks, Dr Crown," Trellis said. "Any more nightmares you'd like to plant in my head? How about telling me that the bogeyman is real?"

"The bogeyman isn't real," Crown said seriously, and picked up a cranium chisel.

"I appreciate that, Doctor," Trellis said, and looked back at the body. "Did she drown?" he asked, still unconvinced that the subject in front of him could have been a person.

"There was water in the air passages, lungs and stomach," Crown said. "And haemorrhaging in the sinuses and lungs, indicating she was alive when she went into the water. I'm doing a complete toxicology examination on her just in case, including the water, to make sure she wasn't drugged."

"I think I hear the printer right now," Trellis said over his shoulder, practically sprinting away from the examination table. Burton was proud of the fact that Trellis hadn't vomited in the examination room yet, but today might be the day.

"Michael," Crown said. "Also check the lab to see if they've processed the water from her lungs."

"Here we go," Trellis said, walking back and concentrating intently on the printer paper.

"The water has normal levels of calcium, magnesium, fluoride and iron, with trace amounts of several other chemicals and elements. The lab also filtered the water from her lungs, and this was what they found." He held up a plastic bag with small particles in it, which Dr Crown took as Trellis tried to focus on anything except the body.

After examining several samples under her comparison microscope, Crown looked at Burton with what he thought might be confusion, but since he'd never seen Dr Crown confused before, he wasn't sure.

"These appear to be small segments of hair," she said. "All about an eighth of an inch long or less."

"Really?" Burton asked. "Her hair?"

"I don't think so," said Crown. "She's a natural brunette, and these are blond with a touch of red."

"Could they be—" Burton began but was interrupted by the examination-room phone. He picked it up and said, "Help! There are a bunch of dead people in here!" Crown shook her head.

"You know, I gave him that idea," Trellis said. "Do you get it? It's because—"

"Yes, I get it," Crown said. "It's because we're in a morgue. Morgues have dead people in them. It might have been humorous the first time, but it decreases in comedic value every time it is uttered."

"Oh," Trellis said. "I guess you do get it."

Burton made a hushing gesture so he could hear the desk sergeant at the other end of the line. "Go ahead, Sergeant," he said.

"Mr Taylor is here with the hairbrush," the desk sergeant said from the reception phone.

"Let me guess," Burton said. "He has strawberry-blond hair and he's clean-shaven."

"That's right, how did you know?" the desk sergeant asked.

"He fits the description of Alyssa's killer," Burton said. "Arrest him."

How did Burton know?

Burton's File

Alyssa Taylor was found in Two Mile Lake, but the water in her lungs contained fluoride, a chemical added to tap water. This meant that she was dumped in the lake after she was dead. The small hairs found in her lungs were her husband's shaving stubble, which had clung to the sides of the bath. When he drowned her in the tub, she inhaled the tap water and enough evidence to convict her killer.

CRIME FILE INVESTIGATIONS

GESUNDHEIT MEANS "YOU'RE GUILTY"

Dr Crown leaned over the body of Gina Reardon on the examining table and spoke clearly for the boom microphone positioned above the work area.

"The marbled appearance of the skin indicates that the subject has been dead for at least four days; however, the presence of blowfly larvae suggests that the body has only been exposed to insects for 16 to 25 hours."

"So Ms Reardon was killed almost a week ago, but her body was kept indoors somewhere until a day ago?" Burton asked.

"That's correct," Crown said. "Insects don't lie." Burton noticed the whimsical way she said it, as if she admired their honesty. He appreciated their contribution to his investigations, but that was about as far as his feelings for insects went.

"Detective Radley was on scene where the body was found," Burton said. "I spoke to her on the phone, and she said there weren't any odd weather factors like extreme cold, so the insect timeline should be correct. The only reason I asked was because she was sneezing uncontrollably. I thought she might be in a freezer or something."

"I see." Crown said. "There is also a mould present on the body and clothing. Toxicology reports indicate that it is Stachybotrys, a type of black mould that typically occurs on materials that contain fibre, such as cardboard and wood, and are constantly wet."

Before she could continue, Mike Trellis poked his head into the examination room. "Hey, boss, they've rounded up the four jokers who were with Gina Reardon just before her disappearance. They were all at the same bar, one female and three males. All friends of hers. Well, except for one, I hope."

"Thanks, Mike," Burton said. "Can you ask Detective Radley to wait for me outside the interview rooms?"

"Sure thing. Do you want her to ask the questions while you give them the stink eye?"

"No, I want to ask them questions while Radley gives them the sniff test."

Why did Burton want Radley to sniff the suspects?

Burton's File

Detective Radley was sneezing over the phone while she was at the dump site of the body. Her sneezing was an allergic reaction to the black mould found on Reardon's body and clothes, which grew there while the body was being kept indoors. Whoever killed Reardon had a bad case of mould infestation at home, and when Radley sniffed the culprit, she started sneezing again. As Mike said after we arrested the killer, Radley was a "nose witness" to the crime.

CRIME FILE INVESTIGATIONS

LYING WITHOUT A NET

Burton approached the interview room and found Mike Trellis standing outside the door, nibbling on his pen. From the look of the plastic cap, Burton guessed it had been going on for quite a while.

"Are you going into the interview room?" Burton asked.

"Nope." Trellis answered.

"Is there a reason why?"

"Clown."

Burton paused. "Pardon me?"

Trellis finally took his eyes off the door and looked at Burton. "There's a clown in there."

"I know," Burton said. "He's Wammo the Clown. He's here for questioning about the death of Mad Kimo Kuhono, the Hawaiian tightrope walker who fell this afternoon. I just talked to the show promoter. He says he's ruined; Mad Kimo was the top attraction, and just about everyone in the stands leaves when his act is over. Now he claims they won't show up at all."

"Don't like clowns," Trellis said, going back to munching on the pen.

"OK," Burton said. "Did you find out what that substance was on the top of Wammo's clown shoes?"

"Black sand," Trellis said, handing the print-out to Burton. "It's unique to Wai'anapanapa State Park in Maui, Hawaii. That's the only place on earth you can find it."

"How did the black sand end up on the tops of Wammo's shoes instead of the soles?" Burton wondered aloud. "It must have fallen onto them."

"He's a clown," Trellis said, staring at the interview room door. "Laws of nature don't apply to him. Have you seen how many of them can fit into a car?"

Burton laughed, since Mike had finally made a good joke, but stopped when he realized that the technician wasn't kidding.

"Is the clown going to stay in there," Trellis asked, "or will he be wandering around scaring innocent technicians?"

"Go to lunch, Mike." Burton said, and entered the interview room. He heard Trellis's running footsteps as he closed the door.

"Hello, Wammo, I'm CSI Wes Burton."

"Hello," said Wammo, who sounded upset despite the huge grin painted on his face.

"Can you go over what happened again?" Burton said. "I just want to make sure I have the facts straight."

"I don't know why you're asking me," said Wammo. "I was in the food tent when Mad Kimo fell."

"I know, but it helps to get viewpoints from anyone in the area. Maybe you saw someone running out of the tent just before Mad Kimo fell?"

"Nope, nothing like that," Wammo said. "From what I heard, Mad Kimo stepped out onto the high wire, went a few steps and started to tip, then overcorrected with his balance pole and fell. They said a big black cloud puffed up when he hit the ground. I can't say for sure. I didn't go into the big top after he fell."

"Wait, back up. The balance pole," Burton said, flipping through his notes. "His partner Whooping Wendy said he made that pole when he was a child and never fell while he was using it. She called it his lucky pole."

"Not lucky enough, I guess," Wammo said, and honked his nose. "Sorry, habit."

"Yeah, I have habits, too." Burton said. "Like this one: You have the right to remain silent... "

How did he know?

Burton's File

A tightrope walker's droopy pole is weighted at each end to lower the walker's centre of gravity. The ends of Kimo's pole, which he built when he was a child in Hawaii, were filled with black sand found only in Maui, the same sand found on top of Wammo's shoes. If Wammo didn't go into the big top after the accident, the only way the sand could have got on to his shoes is if he had let some of it out of the pole before Mad Kimo's act. Wammo was jealous of Mad Kimo's popularity, and he tampered with the balance pole, causing Mad Kimo to fall to his death.

CRIME FILE INVESTIGATIONS

THERE'S NO "FUN" IN "FUNGUS"

"What's the story, Dr Crown?" Burton said as he entered the autopsy room. He snapped on a vinyl glove.

"A story implies fiction. I deal in fact," she responded, without looking up from the body. Mike Trellis, who was assisting on the autopsy, snickered.

"Fair enough," Burton said. "What are the facts?"

"Brenda Thompson, age 43, diabetic. Her husband, Peter Thompson, brought her back from a camping trip after she began to exhibit symptoms of hypoglycemia. She was pronounced dead on arrival this morning at 9.36."

"Low blood sugar?" Burton asked. "Then why does she have signs of jaundice?" He had noticed the yellow shade of her skin as soon as he entered the room.

"That's why I authorized this autopsy," Crown said. "The husband didn't want to allow it, but I saw reasonable doubt about the cause of death."

“Wait a minute,” Burton said. “Peter Thompson. The same Peter Thompson who runs that wilderness camp about 50 miles outside of town? Where the tourists can go and live off the land for a week, as long as they have five grand?”

“That’s him,” said Trellis. “He says they went on the camping trip to make up after a big argument. According to him, Brenda wanted to move back to the city so she could get back to her career. He’s outside raising a fuss about how it’s not natural to open a dead body. He said ‘raccoons don’t do autopsies!’ How does he know?”

Burton and Crown looked at him, then at each other, and shrugged.

“The tissues in her esophagus and mouth are irritated,” Crown continued, “indicating that she vomited recently. Quite violently, from the tissue damage. She’s also severely dehydrated, which supports the vomiting, but that has nothing to do with low blood sugar.”

“Her skin does look pretty dry,” Burton said.

“That’s due in part to these,” Crown said, holding up a box of alcohol wipes. “They used them to clean off; no showers in the wilderness. Good for cleanliness, but bad for moisturizing. Michael, is the blood analysis complete?”

Trellis walked over to the GC/MS equipment and checked the screen, then clicked print. The results of Brenda Thompson’s blood analysis purred out of the printer, and Trellis brought them over to Crown. She quickly found the culprits.

“Amanitin and phalloidin,” she said.

"She was killed by aliens?" Trellis asked.

"Amanitin and phalloidin are poisons," Crown said. "Both are at highly toxic levels in the Amanita phalloides mushroom, better known as the 'death cap.'"

"They sound like real fungis," Trellis said, and looked around the room for applause. There wasn't any. "Get it? Fungis, fun guys?" Burton and Crown turned away from Trellis in an attempt to shut him out of the conversation.

"Did she eat some bad mushrooms by mistake?" Burton asked.

"There were no traces in her stomach or digestive tract," Crown said.

"Could she have barfed them all out?" Trellis asked, earning a stern look from Crown. "Sorry, vomited."

"There would still be traces in her intestines," Crown explained. "We only vomit what's in our stomachs, and amanitin usually takes six to fifteen hours before causing nausea. That's plenty of time for the contents of her stomach to be digested."

"There's a myth about poisonous mushrooms that says you can detoxify them by boiling them in water and vinegar," Burton said. "Any sign of vinegar at the campsite?"

"That myth is nonsense," Crown said. "The only way I've been able to extract the poison is with isopropyl alcohol, and no one would eat a mushroom after it's been soaking in that."

"Alcohol," Burton said. "Mike, tell the officers to arrest Peter Thompson for murder."

How did Burton know?

Burton's File

Peter Thompson was unhappy with his wife because she wanted to move back to the city, ending his business as a wilderness guide. He was familiar with the death cap mushroom and knew that one of its poisons causes hypoglycemia, a condition that can be fatal, especially to those with diabetes. He also knew that the poisons can be extracted using alcohol and that absorbing the tainted mixture through the skin can be as toxic as eating the fungus. He thought the poisoned alcohol wipes he made would allow him to kill his wife and get away clean, but they ended up proving him dirty.

CRIME FILE INVESTIGATIONS

THE TANNING (DEATH) BED

The room was small, and Burton imagined the home owner had a hard time getting the large tanning bed through the door. The bed was now turned off, with the body of Clive Lentil in it. Lentil wore shorts and a set of tanning goggles, which looked like small plastic spectacles. Every inch of exposed skin was bright red.

"Man, I've heard these things are bad for you, but this is out of control," Trellis said, tripping on Burton's foot.

"Hey, watch it," Burton said. "It's like having a meeting in a phone box in here. What did this room used to be, a cupboard?"

"Looks like it," Trellis said. "I don't see any heating vents, so no one was worried about keeping the room warm or cool."

"That's why Lentil used that paraffin heater in the corner," Radley said as she entered. "Mrs Lentil says he kept it running so the bed wouldn't be cold when he got in it. Guess he couldn't wait for the bulbs to warm it up. Ow, that's my elbow."

"Your elbow? What about my ribs?" Trellis said. He would have rubbed the sore spot but didn't have enough room. "So this guy died because he wanted a tan? Cause of death: vanity."

"That may not be the case," Burton said. "There is a condition called seasonal affective disorder; the most common type is also called winter depression. Doctors aren't certain, but it's probably caused by the body's reaction to a lack of sunlight. Some people use tanning beds during the winter months to get a dose of fake sunlight, but it's not a recommended treatment; the UV rays are too strong."

"Great, so now we add clinical depression to the mix," Trellis said. "What's behind door number three, massive gambling debts?"

"You're on my foot again, Mike," Burton sighed.

"Who had garlic for lunch?" Radley asked.

"Sorry," Trellis said.

"OK," Burton said, "Mike, if you've finished taking photos and videos, step outside for a bit. Detective Radley, please see if Mrs Lentil still has the instructions for the tanning bed. I want to see if her husband put in the wrong type of bulbs."

"Got it, boss," Mike said.

"I'll be in the kitchen," said Radley.

Alone, Burton still thought the room was too small to work in, but he'd been in tighter spaces before. He knelt next to the tanning bed and, with a gloved hand, pulled the tanning goggles off of Lentil's face.

The eyelids beneath were the same bright red as the rest of Lentil's skin. Burton put the goggles in an evidence bag from waistcoat pocket 9 and sealed it. He took a close-up photo of the eyelids.

"We might have a problem," Radley said from the doorway.

"No instructions for the tanning bed?"

"Worse. Mrs Lentil's already on the phone with her lawyer, talking about suing the manufacturer for killing her husband."

Burton shook his head. "Tell her to drop that case and start one against the paraffin heater, whoever built this room and Mr Lentil's red blood cells."

How did Lentil die?

Burton's File

While the bright-red colour of Mr Lentil's skin originally indicated that he'd been overexposed to the tanning bed's heat, the fact that his eyelids were also red suggested another cause of death. They would not have been burned with the tanning goggles on. When too much carbon monoxide is inhaled, the body suffocates and bleeding occurs under the skin, resulting in a flushed appearance that is quite similar to a sunburn. In the small, unventilated tanning room, the carbon monoxide created by the paraffin heater would have quickly rendered Mr Lentil unconscious and he suffocated soon after that.

CRIME FILE INVESTIGATIONS

THE SALE OF A LIFETIME

The yellow "CRIME SCENE – DO NOT CROSS" tape was already up when Burton arrived. He reluctantly put his custom-made tape back in waistcoat pocket 2. It sometimes lightened the mood of witnesses and helped them talk about what they had seen. He crossed the car park to a blue four-door sedan with a dead man in the driver's seat.

"Greetings, Detective Radley," he said. She was peering into the driver's window, pointing out areas that she wanted CSI technician Mike Trellis to photograph and video.

"Hello, Burton," she said. "We have one victim, cause of death a gunshot wound to the head." If Radley found the scene disturbing or gross in any way, her voice did not suggest it.

"Do we have the shooter?" Burton asked.

"No, but we do have an eyewitness. The driver was a soap salesman and his passenger was a salesman-in-training." Radley pointed towards a man sitting about 20 yards away on the bumper of a police car. His jacket was off and his tie undone. He had blood smeared across his face and clothes and looked as though standing up would be bad for him.

"The trainee, Daniel Hawes, went to get a takeaway from the deli around the corner while our victim, William Torwell, stayed in the car to do some paperwork," Radley said. "Hawes says he was followed from the deli by a man, and when Hawes got back in the passenger seat, the man approached the driver's window and told Torwell to give him the keys. Torwell refused, so the man shot him and ran away."

"Any good material for your book on why criminals do what they do?" Burton asked her.

"I don't think so," Radley said. "Pretty typical shoot-and-run, if it ends up being like Hawes claims."

"Did Hawes get a good look at the shooter?" Burton asked as he looked into the car.

Radley shook her head. "He said he didn't want to make eye contact with him, so he didn't look at his face."

"Smart, I guess," Burton said. "Some animals, including humans, consider eye contact to be a challenge sometimes." The interior of the car was a mess, with blood spattered onto nearly every surface. The passenger seat and window were covered. The shot had come from the driver's window and the bullet had exited through the back of Torwell's head.

"Where did the bullet end up?" Burton asked.

Torwell was slumped over the steering wheel, but Burton pictured him sitting up when he was shot. "Mike, have you finished taking pictures? I'd like to correct Mr Torwell's posture."

"All set," Trellis said. "I need to take some photos of the paperwork Torwell was filling out anyway, and it's in his lap."

The two of them eased Torwell's body into an upright position, as he would have been at the time of the shooting. Burton found the entrance wound, just above the left ear and inserted a trajectory dowel. The long rod followed the path of the bullet as it entered the skull, indicating the location of the gun barrel. He did the same for the exit wound, the rod extending out and tracing the path of the bullet once it left Torwell's head.

"The bullet was fired from slightly above and in front of Torwell," Burton said. "It exited near the bottom of his skull and went into the back seat. Mike, let's try to recover the slug."

"I'm on it," Trellis said as he put on an extra pair of gloves. "The paperwork is a trainee evaluation form for Hawes. Looks like he wasn't doing very well; Torwell recommended him for warehouse duty."

"There is stippling around the entrance wound, so the gun was within two feet of Torwell's head when it was fired." Burton indicated the small abrasions on Torwell's face and neck. The abrasions were caused by unburned gunpowder and small pieces of metal that exited the gun along with the bullet.

"Must have been loud in the car," Trellis remarked, while he searched the back seat for a bullet hole.

"I agree," Burton said, and turned towards Daniel Hawes. He was still sitting on the car bumper and looking at the ground.

"Mr Hawes?" Burton said at normal conversation volume.

Hawes looked up immediately, still in shock but eager to help out. "Y-yes?"

Burton walked over to the salesman-in-training. The smeared blood on the man's face and clothes made him look even more traumatized. "I'm Wes Burton, CSI. I hope you sell soap better than your story, because I'm not buying it."

How did he know?

Burton's File

Daniel Hawes claimed that he was in the passenger seat when Torwell was shot. If that were true, the passenger seat and window would have been mostly clean rather than completely spattered with Torwell's blood. Hawes did have blood smeared on his face and clothes, but there was no spatter on him, indicating that he was not in the passenger seat when Torwell was shot.

A gunshot is loud, typically around 140 decibels (normal conversation is about 60). A gunshot inside a car is deafening. If Hawes had been in the car when Torwell was shot from less than two feet away, he would not have heard his name from 20 yards away.

Hawes knew that Torwell was giving him a bad review and shot him for it. He dumped the pistol, got into the passenger seat and smeared some blood on himself, then called the police. At least prison doesn't have warehouse duty.

CRIME FILE INVESTIGATIONS

THE DEATH OF THE POTTY

"This is either the cruellest murder," Burton said, "or the dumbest case of accidental death I've ever seen." Burton, Trellis and Detective Gibson were looking into the hunting cabin's outhouse, where the jeans-covered legs of Randy Banks were sticking up out of the toilet. His hunting boots were on his feet, and Burton could clearly read the Lumberland brand name on the soles.

"Either way, something about this case stinks," Trellis said. "Get it? Because of the poop."

"You're fired," Gibson said.

"Don't fire him yet, Frank," said Burton. "We might need someone to go into the outhouse to look for evidence."

"I hope you have a wet suit," Gibson told Trellis, who wasn't laughing anymore. Gibson turned to Burton. "So this guy drops something into the toilet, goes in after it, gets stuck and dies?"

"Pretty much, if that's what happened," Burton said. "Sewer gas is made up of hydrogen sulfide, carbon monoxide and methane. When you inhale it, it takes the place of the oxygen in your blood, and your cells don't get any oxygen. It's a very smelly way to suffocate. We can get a blood sample at the lab. If he has high levels of sulfide, we can conclude he died that way."

"Who found him like this?" Trellis asked.

"One of the other hunters," Gibson said. "There are three more of them in the cabin right now. They said they all had a few beers, went to bed and woke up this morning with no sign of Banks. One of the guys heads for the toilet and finds him like this. Not really the way you want to be remembered."

"What do you think he dropped down there that was so important?" said Trellis.

"Only one way to find out," Burton said. He pulled a filtered mask out of waistcoat pocket 15 and snapped it over his nose and mouth. "Mike, you take the left side, I'll take the right. We need to pull the body up as far as we can, then out." Burton was careful not to slip on the muddy ground outside the outhouse. He was going to get dirty at this scene, but the longer he could put it off, the better.

"Oh, man," Trellis said, also trying not to slip as he entered the outhouse. "If I pass out, you guys have to promise not to take pictures of me."

"I promise," Burton said. Trellis looked at Gibson, who looked back and said nothing.

"OK, on three," said Burton, as he gripped Banks's belt with his right hand and wrapped his left arm around the body's right leg. "One, two, hold it!"

Trellis almost pulled up on the body, let go just in time and stumbled out of the small outhouse into Gibson's arms. Gibson tossed him aside and looked at Burton.

"What is it?" he said.

Burton pointed to the small of Banks's back, where his shirt had been pulled up when Burton grabbed his belt. The skin was a dark purple.

"Hold those three hunters for questioning and seal off the cabin. This man didn't die in the outhouse."

How did Burton know?

Burton's File

The dark purple colour of Banks's back is called lividity, which is caused by gravity pulling blood to the lowest areas of the body after the heart stops. In Randy Banks's case, he was lying on his back when he died, and stayed that way for at least six hours; (if Banks had been rolled onto his left side within those six hours, the blood would have settled there).

If the other hunters were telling the truth, the lividity in Banks's body would have been in his head, arms and shoulders, as those were the lowest parts of his body. In addition, the soles of his hunting boots were clean, even though the ground outside the outhouse was extremely muddy. Banks didn't walk into the outhouse, he was carried. Trellis is right; something does stink about this case.

THE BITTER TASTE OF GUILT

Burton walked into the bar and immediately spotted Detective Radley and Mike Trellis near the group of people being held for questioning. He approached the two of them and asked the bartender for a cup of coffee.

"A man walks into a bar," Trellis said. "He orders a cup of coffee, because it's two in the morning, and then..." he looked at Burton expectantly, waiting for him to finish the joke. Burton did.

"He asks the two people who are already there why he had to get out of bed at 2.00 am for some lady who had her bag stolen in a bar," he said.

"Ha! I love that one!" said Trellis.

"You're here because of what was in the bag," Radley said. "This is Julie Lanier, the owner of the bag." She gestured towards a woman nearby, who stepped into the group.

"Did you find my bag yet?" she asked Burton. The smell of alcohol on her breath was overwhelming.

"It's two in the morning," Burton said. "I haven't even found my face yet. But I did find some breath mints." He took a tin out of waistcoat pocket 11 and offered her one. She took three and managed to get two in her mouth.

"What was in your bag, Miss Lanier, that is causing so much trouble?" Burton asked.

"A great big gun," she said, and pointed her finger at him with her thumb up. "Bang bang!"

"I see," Burton said. "Can you tell me what happened?"

"I can fill you in," Radley said, making Burton very happy. "Miss Lanier was talking to a man in a dark area of the bar. Because of the lighting and her intoxication, she doesn't remember what he looked like and can't pick him out of the group we have over there." Radley pointed to the dozen men standing around the other end of the bar, being watched by two uniformed officers.

"Those guys all look completely different," Burton said. "How can she not pick him out?"

"It was dark, people have to lean way in next to your ear to talk because of the loud music," Trellis said. "You know how it is."

"No, I don't," said Burton. He looked at Radley. "What happened next?"

"The guy she was talking to said something rude, so she threw her drink in his face," Radley said.

"Yeah, I doused him good!" Lanier said. "All over his shirt and everything!"

Radley waited to see if the commentary was done, then continued. "He shoved her back, grabbed her bag off the bar, and took off. The doorman said no one has left the place through the front, and all the other exits are alarmed. So the thief stashed the bag somewhere inside, and he might have the gun on him right now. Problem is, we don't have enough probable cause to search all of them. We need to narrow down the suspect list before we can search anyone."

"Can you smell them?" Burton asked. "Find out which one smells like he had a drink thrown in his face?"

"They all smell that way," Trellis said. "And a few of them smell like they had some wet rubbish thrown in their hair." He looked at the group of men. "It's called a shower, guys!" They smiled and nodded back, having no idea what he said. One of them waved.

"What drink did you throw in his face?" Burton asked Lanier.

"Huh?" she said and wobbled. "Who threw a drink in my face?" Burton frowned.

"I can answer that," the bartender said as she set Burton's coffee down. "Miss Lanier was drinking gin and tonics all night."

"You're absolutely certain of that?" Burton asked.

"Absolutely," the bartender said. "I can print her bill right now."

"Do it," Burton said, and took a small black light out of waistcoat pocket 25. "As for our suspects, line them up. I'll let you know who to question in less than a minute."

How is Burton going to identify the thief?

Burton's File

Miss Lanier threw a gin and tonic on the thief's face and shirt. The bitter taste in tonic water is caused by quinine, a natural product found in the bark of the cinchona tree. Quinine also glows brightly under ultraviolet light, or black light. By scanning the group of men with the UV light, it was easy to find the perpetrator.

CRIME FILE INVESTIGATIONS

THE BATHROOM BRAWL

"I already told you, it was self-defence," Al Williams said, and he was right. He had already told them; four times at the scene, twice in the car and three times since he'd sat down in the interview room. Burton was beginning to wonder if Williams was trying to convince them or himself.

"Definitions of self-defence can vary," Detective Gibson said, pacing behind the seated Williams. "Maybe you thought he was going to pop you in the face, so you hit him first. Or maybe he said he was going to give you a whuppin', so you got scared and threw the first punch."

"No, no," Williams said, shaking his head. "We were in the bathroom arguing over this girl Stacy, and Trevor started to push me, then he hit me in the eye." Williams indicated the swelling there as evidence. "So I blocked the next few strikes – I've had some martial arts training – and punched him in the stomach. That slowed him down, but he was still coming after me, so I kicked him in the head."

"And killed him," Burton added.

"In self-defence," Williams added to that.

"I've never kicked anyone in the head," Gibson said, seeming a bit sad about it. "How do you get your leg that high?"

"Training, like I said." Williams shrugged.

Burton tuned out the circus for a moment and studied the crime scene photographs. One shot taken from the doorway interested him. The deceased Trevor was on the floor of the bathroom. The room measured five feet wide by eight feet long. It was a small room, with the urinal and toilet on the right wall and the sink and paper towel dispenser on the left.

Another image, a close-up of Trevor's head, showed blood spatter on the floor. The drops of blood made dotted "i" shapes pointing away from his head. Burton looked up from the photos to see Gibson taking off Williams's handcuffs.

"Show me how you kicked him," Gibson said, stepping away from the table. Williams stood up and measured the distance between him and Gibson, then made sure he had enough room on the sides. Then his right leg swung from his side in a long arc over the table, and passed about six inches in front of Gibson's face.

"Man, oh, man, that would hurt!" Gibson said, smiling. "So that's the same kind of kick you used on Trevor, with your leg coming around the side like that? What's that called?"

"It's a round kick, or a roundhouse kick, depending on the training," Williams said.

"I hate to interrupt the lesson," Burton said, "but is there a name for kicking someone in the head when they're already on the ground?"

How did Burton know?

Burton's File

The size of the room was the first tip, especially after Williams demonstrated the kick he claimed to have used. The small bathroom would not have allowed him to get his leg fully extended at his side. His foot would have hit the wall or toilet before he hit Trevor.

The bloodstain pattern, a series of dotted "i" shapes, indicated that the blood hit the floor at a small angle, close to 10 degrees. This puts Trevor's head at or near the floor when it was struck. If Trevor had been standing, as Williams claimed, the blood from his wound would have hit the floor at 90 degrees as it dropped, leaving round spatters. Williams knocked Trevor to the floor and then kicked him, a clear case of homicide.

CRIME FILE INVESTIGATIONS

YOU HAVE THE WRITE TO REMAIN SILENT

Burton and Trellis arrived at the bank just before the press did, which made Burton happy. He didn't appreciate having to answer questions when he still had so many himself. Trellis liked being on the news. He claimed his appearances "let the ladies know I'm around".

"Hey, they're giving out free toasters when you open a savings account," Detective Radley said when she spotted them.

"I don't know how to make toast," Burton replied. "What do they give you when you rob the place?"

"A minimum of five years in prison," Radley said. "We have a suspect inside, but he says it wasn't him. Imagine that."

"Hey, Burton, I think I have an artist's sketch of the robber," Trellis said, holding up a fast-food napkin he'd grabbed in the truck. Burton looked at it. It was a crude drawing of a man in a ski mask, his eyes crossed and a speech bubble off to the side that read "Stick 'em up!"

"Get it? Because that's how he looked when he robbed the place," Trellis said.

"Hey, someone wants you over there," Burton said, pointing to the other side of the bank hall.

"Who?"

"Everyone over here," Burton answered and turned to Radley. "Where did they find the suspect?"

"He was out of breath, sitting in a booth at a diner three streets away," Radley said. "The cook called the police when he heard that the bank had been robbed. He noticed that our suspect was wearing long sleeves, long trousers and had a knitted cap sticking out of his pocket in the middle of July."

"He ran from the bank robbery? Guess he didn't buy the right getaway shoes," Trellis said.

"Regardless," said Radley. "He's sticking to his story that it wasn't him. Here's the note the robber used." She handed Burton a plastic bag with a white piece of paper in it. The writing on it was printed by hand.

He read aloud: "'GIVE ME ALL THE MONEY AND NO ONE GETS HURT.' Quick and to the point, I guess," he said. The letters were written in ink. The lines were smeared, but they could still be read. "Let's go and talk to our runner."

The suspect, Shawn Davis, was sitting at the bank manager's desk, surrounded by police officers. Burton sat across from him and introduced himself and Trellis.

"Now, we're going to do a writing exercise," Burton said, pulling a pen out of waistcoat pocket 6 and a pad out of pocket 3. “I’d like you to write the following: Give me all the money and no one gets hurt.”

Davis took the pen in his right hand and spun the paper so that the lower left corner was pointing towards him. He wrote the phrase in cursive, hooking his wrist and sliding the paper from right to left as he went. When he finished, he pushed the sheet back to Burton, a small smile on his lips.

“I’m telling you, you got the wrong guy,” he said.

Burton looked at the writing. It was a barely legible mush. The letters slanted backward, as though they were being pulled at the bottom.

“This looks like ‘Big me att the monkey and no one gels kurl,’” he said, offering it to Trellis, who shook his head.

“It looks like he wrote it with his foot,” he said.

“Is sloppy handwriting a crime?” Davis asked.

“No, but obstructing a criminal investigation is,” Burton answered and slid the pad back to Davis.

“Now write it with your left hand, the one you usually use, and tell me where you stashed the money.”

How did Burton know Davis was left-handed?

Burton's File

At an early age, most left-handers are taught to spin the writing paper slightly counterclockwise so the lower left corner is to the right of their midsection and to slide the paper from right to left as they go, to prevent their left hand from smearing the letters (as in the robbery note). Though this is intended to keep the writer from hooking his or her wrist, if they aren't corrected, many writers will still hook in order to see what they are writing. Also, when a left-handed writer attempts to write like a right-hander, it can result in "backhand" script, where the letters slant backward and become nearly illegible.

Davis showed all of these tendencies when he wrote the note with his right hand, his habits proving he was left-handed, since right-handed writers do not need to make any of those adjustments.

CRIME FILE INVESTIGATIONS

THE CRACKED SAFE CRACKS THE CASE

"Wow, this guy is good. No explosives or torches, and he didn't have to peel the sides off to get in," Burton said. He was examining an open safe in the crime lab, brought in by Trellis and three other helpers.

"What did the owner of the jeweller's say?" Burton asked Detective Radley.

"It was fine when he left work last night, and this is how he found it this morning. His inventory shows that there was close to 500,000 dollars worth of diamonds and other stones in there." Radley, who didn't wear jewellery, sounded insulted that something so small could cost so much.

"So this case won't be making an appearance in your book?" Burton asked.

"I already know the why of this one," Radley muttered. "Greed. We don't need any more insight into why people steal. It's because they're lazy, desperate, cruel and/or have a disorder. Believe it or not, I'm actually more interested in the how for this case."

Burton nodded approvingly, then took a brush out of waistcoat pocket 16 and silver latent print powder out of pocket 22 and began dusting the door of the safe for fingerprints, knowing that there wouldn't be any. A safecracker this good would definitely wear gloves, probably two pairs. A series of whorls did appear near the dial, but it was too big to be a fingerprint.

"We do have a Mr Horace Dubois in custody," Radley said. "An eyewitness saw him leaving the building around three this morning."

"What kind of eyewitness is out and about at that time of night?" Burton asked. "A vampire?"

"No, she's an early shift waitress at a diner across the street from the jeweller's," Radley said. "She said the guy had been spending time in the restaurant, drinking coffee and writing in a notebook. She thought he was some kind of author, then she sees him leaving the jeweller's at three in the morning. When she saw the police there around six, she flagged one of the officers down and told him what she saw. I showed her some photos of known safecrackers, and she picked out Horace right away."

"Sounds pretty good," Burton said.

"Yeah, except she won't testify," Radley said, not bothering to hide her disgust.

"Don't tell me," Burton said, still looking at the safe. "She doesn't want the Mafia to come after her."

"Too many movies, too much TV," said Radley. "She thinks she's going to need witness protection, relocation, plastic surgery, new shoes... I told her that Horace was working alone, otherwise he wouldn't have been walking away from the jeweller's."

"And she still won't testify?" Burton asked.

"Not a chance. We were lucky to get her to come down and look at the photos. I had to let her wear my coat and motorcycle helmet as a disguise."

"Maybe we don't need her," Burton said. "I'm going to fume this safe with cyanoacrylate. Can you give me a hand rolling it into the booth?"

He and Radley rolled the safe into the plastic tank. Burton placed a few drops of superglue into the tiny dish on top of the tank's heater. He closed the airtight door and turned on the heater and small fans inside the tank. Once the glue reached the boiling point, its fumes circulated throughout the tank and stuck to any trace of amino acids, fatty acids, sweat, or other substances left behind by human touch.

"There we go," Burton said, pointing to the whorls he'd spotted earlier. The glue's fumes had found them as well, creating a sticky white material along the ridges of the seashell-shaped print. "Don't save a seat for this evidence; it'll be standing up in court."

"That looks a little big for a fingerprint," Radley said.

"Who said anything about a finger?" Burton replied, and headed for the interview room, his digital camera in hand.

"Hello, Horace," he said. "I'm here to take your picture for the mug shot yearbook." He walked around the table to Horace's left side. "Face front please," he said. When Horace did, Burton took a close-up of his left profile and headed for the door.

"Don't you want a shot of my pretty face, too, before I ditch this place?" Horace asked.

"I'll see enough of that in court," Burton said, and closed the door.

Why did he want a shot of Horace's profile?

Burton's File

Horace Dubois was very careful to avoid leaving fingerprints behind, but he didn't think about another unique body part that could identify him: his ear. When he pressed against the safe's door to hear the lock tumblers, he left a perfect print of his left ear, a body feature that scientists have shown is never duplicated.

CRIME FILE INVESTIGATIONS

THE RULES OF DROOL

"Your dog ate my cake," Scott said.

"Yeah, she's in trouble," Danny added. Burton's nephews were out of breath from running over to give him this news. The family reunion had been pretty uneventful until now. Burton considered Uncle Stan's belch at the dinner table the highlight.

"Are you sure?" he asked the boys.

"Yup," said Danny, the younger of the two. Both of the boys were dirty from playing, but the dirt on Danny's good trousers was serious enough to cause problems when his mum saw it. "We were playing catch, and I threw the ball over the fence. Scott went to get it, and when he got back the cake was gone."

"What kind of cake was it?" Burton asked.

"Chocolate with chocolate icing," Scott said. He sounded like he'd lost a close friend.

"If she did eat it, we need to get it out of her

stomach," Burton said, already moving. "Chocolate is very bad for dogs. She could die from eating it."

"Really?" Danny asked, jogging to keep up. "What does she have for dessert?"

"Oh, green beans, pumpkin, sometimes a beef tendon. It depends," Burton said.

"Gross," said Danny and Scott.

In the back garden, Burton found Ed lying under the picnic table. There was a white paper plate face up on the ground, but she seemed more interested in a bee that was buzzing around her tail.

"Come here, Ed," Burton said. She trotted over to him, tail swishing, and sat at his feet as he knelt down. He checked her teeth and gums for traces of chocolate.

"I don't see anything," he said to the boys. "No grass either. Some dogs will eat grass to make themselves vomit."

"Gross," said Scott again.

"How come cows don't throw up when they eat grass?" Danny asked.

"Where do you think milk comes from?" Burton said.

"Ohhh! Nasty!" The boys almost fell on the ground giggling.

"I'll be right back. Ed, you stay," Burton said. He returned from his truck with a bottle of hydrogen peroxide and a miniature ultraviolet light. The boys were pretending to eat grass, throw up, then drink it. Ed was blinking and enjoying the warm sun on her back, sticking out her pink tongue.

Burton went to the paper plate and knelt. There were a few cake crumbs still attached and a streak of icing near the edge. He switched on the UV light and ran it over the plate, the fluorescent bulb about an inch above the surface.

"What are you doing?" Scott asked, forgetting about his cow imitation.

"Dried body fluids will light up when illuminated with UV light, except blood, which looks black," Burton said. "If there is any saliva on this plate, it will glow when I run this light over it."

"I see some right there!" Danny said, pointing towards the plate.

"That's icing," Burton said.

"What about that?" Danny asked, his finger moving across the plate.

"That's a piece of leaf," answered Burton.

"Hey! Get away!" Danny burst out, jumping back from the plate. Ed's friend the bee was buzzing next to Danny's trouser leg, trying to land on his dirt stain. Scott ran to the other side of the picnic table.

"Get away, bee!" Danny yelled, swiping at the insect.

"Don't swat at it," Burton said softly. "You'll only scare him." He brought the UV light over to the bee, which drifted away from Danny and towards the light.

"Bees are attracted to ultraviolet light," Burton said. "Some flowers have patterns that are only visible under UV light. The patterns help the bees find the centre of the flower, where the pollen and nectar are." He slowly took the light over to a flower bed, where the bee landed on a sunflower and got to work.

"So," he said, switching off the light. "Danny, I think you owe Ed an apology, and your brother a piece of chocolate cake."

How did Burton know Danny ate the cake?

Burton's File

The crumbs and icing on the plate were the first indicators that Ed did not eat the cake. A dog would have licked the plate clean, leaving no crumbs and plenty of saliva behind. The UV test showed no saliva on the plate.

The stain on Danny's trousers, originally thought to be dirt, was chocolate. Danny wiped his hands after he ate the cake. The bee detected the sugar and buzzed in for a closer look. Danny waited until Scott left to retrieve the ball that went over the fence, then ate his piece of cake.

CRIME FILE INVESTIGATIONS

THE SHOCKING TRUTH

When Burton arrived at the construction site, Detective Radley already had the electricians sitting in the break area. Don Evans, master electrician, lay two storeys up from where they sat. He had stepped off a two-man lift and fallen 67 feet, dying upon impact. Radley met Burton before he reached the group of men.

"They're all pretty upset," she said. "It's dangerous work, and something like this doesn't make it any easier. Especially when it happens to someone like Evans, who's been doing it for 20 years."

"So he just jumped?" Burton asked.

Radley flipped her notebook open. "Witnesses say at around 8.45 am – they know the time because that's 15 minutes before break – Evans was in the two-man lift with Kevin Randolph. They were working on a 100-amp electrical panel. Randolph said that Evans jumped back from the panel, said

'Not again!' and went over the side. Randolph said it happened so fast, he couldn't tell if Evans fell or jumped."

"Did Evans and Randolph have any history, any problems with each other?" Burton asked.

Radley shook her head. "In fact, Randolph was Don Evans's apprentice. They were good friends. I asked Randolph to wait in the contractor's office. Let's go and see what else he has to say."

Kevin Randolph absently sipped at a cup of water, his eyes not quite focused on anything. "We wanted to get that panel done before break, so we were working faster than we should have," he said, shaking his head slowly. "We would have started earlier, but Baxter needed to use Don's mobile phone."

"Who is Baxter?" Radley asked, her pen ready.

"Jordan Baxter, he's an electrician, too. He has a mobile phone, but the reception stinks up there, and he didn't want to walk all the way back down here. He always complains about the way Don's phone rings; it's the theme from that Yeah, Baby! movie. So Don gave him a hard time about using a phone that he gripes about all the time. We could have started on that panel ten minutes earlier if Baxter hadn't used Don's phone."

"You heard Mr Evans say 'Not again' before he fell," Radley said. "Any idea what that meant?"

"He probably got shocked again. But I didn't hear anything or smell any burn," Randolph said.

"'Shocked again'?" Radley repeated. "Mr Evans had been shocked before?"

"Oh yeah," Randolph said. "One time really badly.

Put him in the hospital for a couple of days. You can't do this for 20 years and not get burned a few times. I've been hit four times already, and it's only my third year."

"You might want to look into plumbing," Burton said. Randolph cracked a smile, his first since the interview started.

"Thank you for your time, Mr Randolph. If you could wait here a bit longer, we're going to tend to Mr Evans," Radley said, shaking Randolph's hand.

Two floors up, Burton and Radley took pictures and videos of Evans's body, including his tools, which were scattered as far as 20 feet. Burton saw the top of a mobile phone poking out of a pocket on Evans's right leg. As he leaned in for a photo, the phone buzzed to life, startling the CSI.

"Do you not hear what I don't hear?" Burton asked Radley.

"I don't hear the Yeah, Baby! theme, if that's what you mean. Why would he set his phone to vibrate if he enjoyed how much the ring annoyed Baxter?" she wondered.

Burton extracted the phone from the pocket with gloved hands and waited until the caller hung up or was sent to voice mail. He hoped it was a telemarketer; Mr Evans had just made it onto the ultimate do-not-call list.

He opened the phone's flip face and scrolled through the recent calls. There was one call at 8.46 am, approximately the time Evans had fallen.

"Let's go downstairs," Burton said. "I have a quick call to make."

Standing out of earshot of the electricians, Burton redialled the number of the 8.46 phone call. One of the men looked at his phone and answered.

"Hello?"

"Jordan Baxter?"

"Yes?"

"This is CSI Wes Burton. You're under arrest for murder. Would you be interested in one free phone call and a terrible lawyer?"

How did he know?

Burton's File

Jordan Baxter borrowed Don Evans's phone before Evans fell. Annoyed with the ring and angry with Evans for teasing him, Baxter switched the phone to the vibrate setting before returning it to Evans. As Kevin Randolph said, every electrician gets shocked, and Baxter knew that a bad shock begins with a vibrating sensation. Don Evans had been shocked badly before. When Baxter called him at 8.46, knowing he was working with dangerous levels of electricity, Evans thought he was getting shocked again when he felt the phone vibrate. He jumped away from the panel, falling to his death.

CRIME FILE INVESTIGATIONS

DID THE BOA CAUSE THE DOA?

The apartment smelled like cheese, beer and cheap cologne, and Burton immediately knew who lived there.

"College students," he said to Detective Gibson.

"That's right," Gibson said. "We have Dennis Fuller, the deceased, in his bedroom. The other guy who lives here, Wayne Collins, found him on the floor. Looks to me like he's been asphyxiated."

"Choked on something, or strangled?" Burton asked.

"Snake," said Gibson.

"Beg your pardon?"

"Collins said that Fuller's own snake killed him. It's a boa constrictor," Gibson said. Burton thought he saw the big man shiver.

"Did the boa kill him?" Burton asked.

"If I knew that, why would you be here?" Gibson said.

"Frank," Burton said. "Are you saying that you admire me?"

"Like I admire taxes," said Gibson. "They're necessary, but I don't have to enjoy them."

"That's sweet," said Burton. "What did Collins have to say?"

Gibson flipped open his notebook. "Collins says he got home about an hour ago, watched some TV and went to take a shower. He couldn't find his towel, and since Fuller was always taking the towel because he never washed his own, Collins went into Fuller's room to look for it. He found Fuller on the floor and called for an ambulance." Gibson closed the notebook and looked at Burton expectantly, like he was waiting for him to solve the scene right then.

"I might need to look at the body," Burton said.

"Whatever, be my guest," said Gibson. "I'll be out here."

Burton took his CRIME SEEN? tape out of waistcoat pocket 2 and rolled it across the apartment doorway, then went into the bedroom. Fuller was sprawled facedown in the middle of the room. The clutter of CDs, incense burners and dirty clothes on the floor would make it difficult to determine which items were evidence. Burton was not looking forward to bagging everything as he snapped photos and took a video of the scene. When he was finished, Gibson leaned in the doorway, his eyes checking every corner three times.

"Frank," Burton said. "Where is the boa constrictor right now?"

"Yeah, that. We're not real sure where it is. I'll be outside," Gibson said.

"Hold on," Burton said. "I need help rolling him over." Gibson took another five looks around the room, then stepped in like it was a minefield. He hurried over to Burton, and together they rolled Fuller onto his back.

"OK, see ya," Gibson said.

"Wait," said Burton, barely hiding his smile. He looked into Fuller's eyes and saw small red dots in the white areas. "He has petechial haemorrhaging, so strangulation was probably the cause of death."

"Yeah, we knew that. Bye bye," Gibson tried again.

"But look at this," Burton said, pointing to Fuller's throat. "He has a pattern imprinted on his neck. It looks like a spiral, and it goes across the front and sides, but not the back. I don't see any abrasions, so it was made by something soft."

"Like slimy snake scales?" Gibson said, his voice getting high.

"Snakes aren't slimy," Burton said. "But murdering roommates are. We need to find that towel."

Why did Burton want the towel?

Burton's File

Boa constrictors do kill their prey by suffocation, but they wrap themselves around the chest of their victim and tighten with each breath, making it impossible for the prey to inhale. The throat does not expand and contract while a person is breathing, so the snake would not choose to wrap itself around that area of the body. The imprints on Fuller's throat did not continue to the back of his neck; if the snake had choked him, the imprint would have wound all the way around his neck, allowing the boa to squeeze. Those imprints, combined with the spiral marks in them, indicate that Fuller was strangled from behind by a twisted piece of soft fabric. Perhaps a dirty bath towel?

CRIME FILE INVESTIGATIONS

GLOSSARY

Abrasion When skin is worn or rubbed away.

Accelerant A flammable material used to start a fire.

Asphyxiate To die from a lack of oxygen to the brain.

Autopsy The examination of a corpse to determine or confirm the cause of death.

Blood spatter The pattern of blood deposits at a crime scene that can help determine what occurred at the scene.

Compress To press or squeeze.

Convict (noun) A person found guilty of an offence or crime.
(verb) To prove someone guilty of a crime in court.

Cranium The skull.

Cyanoacrylate Also known as superglue, it is fumed over substances to reveal fingerprints.

Deceased A body that is no longer living.

Decompose When a body starts to decay or break down after death.
DNA The molecule that carries the genetic information in the cell. Traces of DNA from saliva, skin, blood and other sources can be used to identify the person who left the trace.
EMT Emergency medical technician.
Evidence Any physical item that assists in proving or disproving a conclusion. For example, a paint scraping is evidence; an eyewitness account is not.
Gas chromatograph/mass spectrometer (GC/MS) A system of instruments used to separate a complex mixture and identify its components.
Glucose The main circulating sugar in the blood and the major energy source of the body.
GSR Gunshot residue, the trace materials left behind when a gun is fired.
Haemorrhage A rapid and sudden loss of blood.
Homicide The killing of one person by another.
Hypoglycemia An abnormally low level of glucose in the blood.
Laceration A jagged wound or cut.
Lividity The discolouration of the skin caused by the settling of blood that occurs in a body after the heart stops.
Marbled Patterned with veins or streaks of colour resembling marble.
Postmortem Occurring after death.
Stippling The deposit of unburned powder and other gunshot residue on a bullet wound. It can help determine the distance between the shooter and the victim.

Toxicology The analysis of poisons and drugs in the blood and body fluids.

Trace element A very small bit of chemicals or evidence.

Trajectory The path of an object moving through the air.

UV light Ultraviolet light, also known as black light, is used to identify many trace evidence items such as body fluids, drugs and inks.